Eugenia Lincoln and the Unexpected Package

Books for early readers

FROM KATE DICAMILLO AND CHRIS VAN DUSEN

Mercy Watson

Mercy Watson to the Rescue

Mercy Watson Goes for a Ride

Mercy Watson Fights Crime

Mercy Watson: Princess in Disguise

Mercy Watson Thinks Like a Pig

Mercy Watson: Something Wonky This Way Comes

Tales from Deckawoo Drive

Leroy Ninker Saddles Up

Francine Poulet Meets the Ghost Raccoon

Where Are You Going, Baby Lincoln?

Eugenia Lincoln and the Unexpected Package

Volume Four

Eugenia Lincoln and the Unexpected Package

Kate DiCamillo
illustrated by Chris Van Dusen

CANDLEWICK PRESS

This is a work of fiction. Names, characters, places, and incidents are either products of the author's imagination or, if real, are used fictitiously.

First paperback edition 2018

Library of Congress Catalog Card Number 2017956975
ISBN 978-0-7636-7881-4 (hardcover)
ISBN 978-1-5362-0353-0 (paperback)

18 19 20 21 22 23 BVG 10 9 8 7 6 5 4 3 2 1

Printed in Berryville, VA, U.S.A.

This book was typeset in Mrs. Eaves.
The illustrations were done in gouache.

Candlewick Press
99 Dover Street
Somerville, Massachusetts 02144

visit us at www.candlewick.com

For Karla Marie

K. D.

To Kate—

It's an honor to illustrate your words

C. V.

Chapter One

Eugenia Lincoln was a practical person, a sensible person. She did not have time for poetry, geegaws, whoop-de-whoops, or frivolity.

She believed in attending to the task at hand.

Eugenia Lincoln believed in Getting Things Done.

Baby Lincoln, Eugenia's younger sister, loved poetry, geegaws, and whoop-de-whoops of every sort and variety.

She was especially fond of frivolity.

"We are diametrically opposed," said Eugenia to Baby. "You are woefully impractical. I am supremely practical."

"Yes, Sister," said Baby.

"You are soft, and I am sharpened to a very fine point, indeed," said Eugenia.

"Well, yes," said Baby. "That's true, I suppose."

"Suppose nothing," said Eugenia. "Believe me when I say that your head is in the clouds, and my feet are planted firmly on the terra firma."

"If you say so, Sister," said Baby.

"I say so," said Eugenia.

And that is how it was with Eugenia Lincoln and Baby Lincoln.

Until the day the unexpected package arrived.

• • •

"Package for Eugenia Lincoln," said the deliveryman.

"I am Eugenia Lincoln," said Eugenia. "But I am not expecting a package."

"Well, whether you are expecting it or not," said the deliveryman, "it's here." He smiled a very big smile.

"Oh, my," said Baby Lincoln, "an unexpected package." She clapped her hands together. "How entirely, absolutely unexpected! Aren't you surprised, Eugenia? *I* am certainly surprised. Isn't it exciting?"

"There's nothing exciting about it," said Eugenia. "It's annoying. It's inconsiderate. People should not send unexpected packages." General Washington, Eugenia's cat, brushed up against the side of the box in a possessive way.

THIS SIDE
UP

"Mooooowwwwlll," he said.

"Stop that," said Eugenia to the cat.

She stared down at the package.

"I refuse," said Eugenia.

"What?" said the deliveryman. He was wearing a name tag that said I'M FASSSST. I'M FREDERICK.

"I refuse to accept delivery, Frederick," said Eugenia.

Frederick stopped smiling. He said, "Hold up there. Are you Eugenia Lincoln?"

"I am," said Eugenia.

"Is this fifty-two Deckawoo Drive?"

"It is," said Eugenia.

"Then this here is your package," said Frederick. "And that's the end of that particular story."

He gave the package a pat, tipped his hat, and then walked down the sidewalk to his delivery truck, whistling as if he didn't have a care in the world.

Frank, who lived at 50 Deckawoo Drive, came over as soon as the deliveryman left. He said, "I see you have received a large package, Miss Lincoln. May I be of some assistance?"

"Yoo-hoo," called Mrs. Watson, who lived at 54 Deckawoo Drive. "Whatever could be in that extremely large box?"

"I have no idea," said Eugenia.

"Just one second," said Mrs. Watson. "Mercy and I will come over and see."

"Do not come over here!" shouted Eugenia. "And do not bring that pig!"

But it was too late. Mrs. Watson and her pig were already out the door and on their way.

"It's all so unexpected," said Baby, "isn't it, Sister? I, for one, have never been so surprised. Why don't you open the package and see what's inside?"

Eugenia put her hands on her hips. She stared down at the box. She was very, very annoyed. She had things to do. She did not have time for an oversize, unexpected package.

"I wonder if there's something dangerous inside," said Frank.

"Don't be ridiculous," said Eugenia.

"Maybe someone sent you something to eat," said Mrs. Watson. "Maybe it's a fruit basket."

"Who would send me a fruit basket?" said Eugenia.

The pig snuffled the box.

"The return address says the Blizzintrap Schmocker Company," said Frank. "What is the Blizzintrap Schmocker Company?"

"I have no idea," said Eugenia.

The pig oinked. It snuffled the box some more.

Life was too annoying and unpredictable and pig-filled to be borne, sometimes. That was Eugenia's general feeling.

"Open it, open it," trilled Mrs. Watson.

"I think you should open it, Sister," said Baby. "I have a feeling that it is something wondrous."

"What a ridiculous feeling to have," said Eugenia Lincoln.

But then, entirely against her better judgment, Eugenia bent down and began to open the unexpected package.

SIDE
UP

Chapter Two

Eugenia cut through the tape. She dug through the packing material.

"What in the world could it be?" said Baby. She clapped her hands. "Oh, it is so exciting! And also very unexpected."

"It's terribly exciting," said Mrs. Watson. "I am hoping that it is a fruit basket. Maybe it will contain oranges and bananas and perhaps a gigantic pineapple or two. Mercy loves a fruit basket."

It was not a fruit basket.

It was an accordion.

Baby and Eugenia and Mrs. Watson and Frank and the pig and General Washington all stood together and stared down at the opened box.

"It's an accordion," said Frank.

"Obviously," said Eugenia.

"I was hoping for a fruit basket," said Mrs. Watson.

"Yes," said Eugenia. "You said so. Several times."

"Well, an accordion is a wonderful thing. It's almost as wonderful as a fruit basket," said Mrs. Watson. "Mercy just adores a fruit basket."

"Who cares what pigs adore?" said Eugenia. She stood with her hands on her hips and considered the accordion. She couldn't think of anything more frivolous, more geegaw-esque, more whoop-de-whoop-ish than an accordion.

Except perhaps a fruit-basket-adoring pig.

"I guess I'll head on home now," said Mrs. Watson.

"Good," said Eugenia. "Take that pig with you."

Mrs. Watson left.

The pig, however, stayed behind.

Eugenia closed her eyes. She didn't have time to deal with a pig. Little men with feathers in their caps were dancing through her head playing accordions and shouting "Oompah, oompah!"

Eugenia Lincoln did not believe in shouting "Oompah!"

Nor did she believe in putting a feather in one's cap.

She opened her eyes. "Franklin," she said, "tell me again the name of the company imprinted on the box."

"Blizzintrap Schmocker," said Frank.

"Located where?" said Eugenia.

"New York City," said Frank.

"Right," said Eugenia. "I will have this straightened out in no time."

"But Sister," said Baby. "It seems like such a nice accordion. Maybe someone wants you to have it. Maybe there is a reason you received it."

"Nonsense," said Eugenia. "There is absolutely no reason for me to receive an accordion."

Eugenia marched to the phone. She dialed information. "I need the number for a Blizzintrap Schmocker Company in New York City," said Eugenia. "Connect me immediately."

A very long way away, a phone rang. "Blizzintrap Schmocker Company," said an annoyingly sweet voice. "This is Gladys Schmocker speaking. How may I help you?"

"Yes," said Eugenia. "I have inadvertently been sent an accordion, and I would like to return it forthwith."

"Oh, my," said Gladys in her too-sweet voice. "I'm afraid that can't be done."

"Of course it can be done," said Eugenia. "All things can be done if one just applies oneself."

"All of our accordions are non-returnable, you see," said Gladys.

"I don't see," said Eugenia. "I don't see at all. You can't stop me from returning it. I am sending it back to you right this very moment."

"Well," said Gladys. "You can send it back. But we will just return it to you. We are duty-bound to do so. Accordions belong with their people."

"I am not," said Eugenia, "this accordion's people. Or person. Or what have you."

"Accordions can enrich your life in unexpected ways," said Gladys. "They are doorways to the soul."

"Doorways to the soul?" sputtered Eugenia. She slammed down the phone.

She had never been so frustrated in her life.

Actually, this was not true.

Eugenia spent a large portion of her life being frustrated. It was hard not to be frustrated. The world was just so . . . frustrating. It refused to bend. It refused to be reasonable, sensible.

For instance, life presented you with accordions when the last thing you wanted was an accordion.

"Are you okay, Miss Lincoln?" said Frank. "Your face is very red."

"I am perfectly fine," said Eugenia.

This was a lie, of course, but under the circumstances, it seemed entirely appropriate to fib.

Chapter Three

"What did the accordion company say, Sister?" said Baby.

"Something idiotic about how accordions are doorways to the soul," said Eugenia.

"Fascinating," said Baby. "I have also heard that accordions can be a pathway to great joy."

"Joy!" said Eugenia. She snorted. And then she narrowed her eyes. "What exactly do you know about this accordion, Baby Lincoln?"

"Nothing," said Baby. "Why would I know a thing about an accordion?" She cleared her throat. "I know exactly nothing about this accordion, or any other accordion."

"That had better be true," said Eugenia. She walked past Baby. She went into the living room and saw that the pig from next door had invited itself into the house and was now sitting on the couch and staring into space as if it were thinking, which it most certainly was not.

"Get off the couch immediately!" Eugenia shouted.

The pig looked at her and then looked away. Eugenia felt light-headed. The world made no sense. How could a pig sit on a couch in one's own home? How could you not return an accordion?

"Maybe you should sit down, Miss Lincoln," said Frank.

"I'm fine," said Eugenia. "I just need to make a list."

Eugenia Lincoln was very fond of lists. They helped her think. Lists calmed her. They made the world seem orderly and reasonable and manageable, even though the world was none of those things.

Frank led Eugenia to the chair across from the pig. "Sit down here," he said. "I will get you a piece of paper and a pencil."

Eugenia looked over at the accordion. It was sitting in the hallway; its keys were gleaming in a malevolent way.

"Sister?" said Baby. She poked her head into the room.

"I am thinking," said Eugenia. "Don't disturb me."

"Yes, Sister," said Baby. "I will go away."

Frank returned with a glass of water and a pad of paper and a pencil. "Drink the water," said Frank. "It will calm you down."

"I am perfectly calm," said Eugenia. But she drank the water anyway.

And then she took the pencil and the paper and wrote *Possible Courses of Action Re: The Accordion.* She underlined the words.

She thought for a moment and then she wrote:

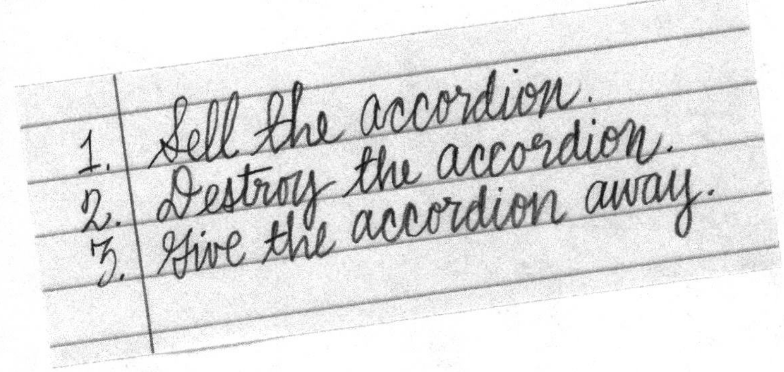

Frank looked over her shoulder. "Those are all good ideas, Miss Lincoln," he said.

"I know," said Eugenia. She tapped the pencil against her teeth.

"You could also just, um, keep the accordion," said Frank.

"Not an option," said Eugenia.

She looked up from her list and stared at the accordion. Its white keys were glowing in the late afternoon light coming in through the front door. It looked extremely determined.

“Miss Lincoln,” said Frank. “Don’t you want to know who sent you the accordion?”

Eugenia felt a small ping of uncertainty. It was the ping of the unknown, the unexplainable. Eugenia did not care for such pings.

“I do not want to know,” said Eugenia.

"It's very mysterious, isn't it?" said Frank in a dreamy voice. "Whenever I want to find out more about something, I look it up in the encyclopedia."

"I do not believe in the mysterious," said Eugenia. "And in this instance, the encyclopedia would be no help at all."

Baby came into the living room and said, "Wouldn't it be divine if you learned how to play the accordion, Eugenia? Wouldn't it be joyous?"

"Would you please stop talking about accordions and joy?" said Eugenia. "I have absolutely no desire to learn how to play an accordion."

Baby sighed.

"For heaven's sake, Baby," said Eugenia. "Why don't you make yourself useful?

Go over to the Watsons' and tell them to remove their pig from my house. In the meantime, I will call the *Gizzford Gazette.*"

"Yes, Sister," said Baby. She sighed again.

Eugenia went into the kitchen. She dialed the phone.

"Good afternoon," she said. "I would like to place an ad in the classifieds under the heading Items for Sale. Yes. Yes. Thank you. I would like for the copy to read: For Sale, Brand-New Accordion. Never Used. Reasonable Price. Inquire at Fifty-Two Deckawoo Drive."

Eugenia felt much better. Decisions had been made. Action had been taken. The accordion and its glowing keys would soon be gone. That would teach them (whoever *they* were) to send her an unexpected package.

She walked back into the living room.

Frank was in the chair reading Volume *U–V* of the encyclopedia.

The pig was still sitting on the couch.

"I should put an ad in the paper for you," said Eugenia to the pig.

The pig ignored her.

Without looking up from the encyclopedia, Frank said, "Mr. and Mrs. Watson would be very upset if you tried to sell Mercy."

"And more is the pity," said Eugenia.

Chapter Four

The next day, there was a knock at the door.

Eugenia opened it and discovered a small, round man. The man was wearing a green velvet suit and a green velvet hat. The hat resembled a moldy mushroom.

"Yes?" said Eugenia.

The man removed the velvet mushroom from his head and bowed deeply. "I am Gaston LaTreaux."

"Good for you," said Eugenia.

"I have come about the accordion," said Gaston. He put the mushroom back on his head and smiled. The man had a large number of teeth. More teeth than the average person, it seemed. Eugenia felt it would be dangerous to trust such an excessively toothy person. But still, she had an accordion to sell. She couldn't afford to be overly particular.

"I have here a card to prove my worth," said Gaston. He smiled at her. He took the hat off his head and put it back on again. He removed a stack of cards from somewhere deep in his velvet pants.

"A card is not necessary," said Eugenia.

Gaston LaTreaux thumbed through the cards. "But it will show you exactly who I am," he said. "Everything is very good. All is just exactly as it should be."

"I doubt that most sincerely," said Eugenia.

Baby appeared. She said, "Oh, we have a visitor. Isn't that wonderful?"

"Hello, beautiful lady," said Gaston to Baby. "I greet you with excessive amounts of joy." He took the hat off his head. He bowed deeply. The stack of cards fluttered to the ground.

"For pity's sake," said Eugenia.

"You should not worry," said Gaston. He smiled at her with his many teeth.

He put his hat back on and bent to pick up the cards. "I will find the card for you."

"As I said previously, I do not need a card," said Eugenia. She could feel her face getting warm.

"Ah, but I have located it," said Gaston. "Here it is, the card of my worth!" He handed a card to Eugenia.

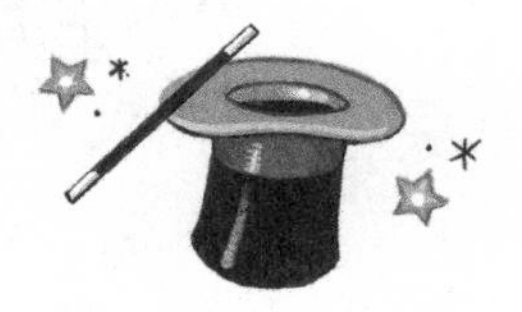

Magic tricks of every variety.
Parties large and small.

She lowered the card. “I have absolutely no need for magic,” she said. “And I am not throwing a party.”

“Wrong card, wrong card. Wait just a moment, please,” said Gaston. He shuffled through the cards. “Yes, yes. I have found it. Please, read it.” Gaston reached past Eugenia and handed a card to Baby.

Joyous exhalations.

Songs for every occasion.

Composed and sung for you by Gaston.

Baby smiled. “Isn’t that just wonderful? I do love a good song.”

"So sorry," said Gaston. "This is not the card I am searching for, either."

"No one needs a card!" said Eugenia. She stamped her foot. "Let us attend to the matter at hand. There is an accordion for sale. Do you wish to purchase it or not?"

"Ah, please hold for only a minute," said Gaston. "I have located it. Here is the correct card. You will see." He handed another card to Eugenia.

Accordion lessons.

Gaston LaTreaux can teach anyone
to make beautiful sounds
upon the world's most magnificent instrument.

Eugenia lowered the card. She felt, as usual, extremely frustrated. Why was everyone so annoyingly obtuse? "I do not want accordion lessons," she said. She spoke slowly. "I have an accordion. For sale. I am selling an accordion. Do you. Wish to. Purchase it?"

"Ho, ho, ho," said Gaston, as if Eugenia had just told him some very funny joke.

At this point, Frank showed up. "Hello, Miss Lincoln," he said to Eugenia. "Hello, Miss Lincoln," he said to Baby. "I was thinking that I might study your encyclopedias some more today."

"Young, noble sir," said Gaston. "I greet you. I salute your pursuit of the knowledge." He took his mushroom off his head. He bowed.

"Hello," said Frank.

"I have arrived to teach the lady, the taller one—the grim one—how to play the accordion."

"Really?" said Frank.

"I beg your pardon," said Eugenia. "That is patently untrue. No one is going to teach me anything."

"You will have a card, of course," said Gaston. "You must."

"Thank you," said Frank. He took a card. *"Winged journeys with Gaston—an inquiry into the migration of the butterflies."* He looked up and smiled. "Wow," he said. "I've always wanted to know more about butterfly migration."

"At your service," said Gaston. He raised his velvet hat and lowered it. "But first, we must turn our attention to the accordion."

And then, somehow, the little man made his way through the door and into the Lincoln Sisters' house.

How, exactly, this was allowed to happen was a mystery to Eugenia.

It was also extremely frustrating.

Chapter Five

They were in the kitchen.

Gaston had the accordion strap around his neck. His velvet mushroom hat was on the table.

"So you see," said Gaston. "It is a simple affair. You put the accordion around your neck and then depress the keys and squeeze the box, and the music arrives—voilà!"

Gaston closed his eyes. He squeezed the accordion. He depressed some keys. A small, sweet melody came into the world.

"Oh, how wonderful," said Baby. She clapped her hands.

"Yes, yes," said Gaston. "Everyone must clap. Everyone must clap along because we are all playing the music."

Frank clapped. Baby clapped.

Eugenia did not clap.

Gaston LaTreaux's accordion playing got louder.

General Washington looked up at Eugenia. ***"Moowwwwwllll?"*** he said. And then he left the room with his tail high in the air.

"I am interested in selling this instrument!" shouted Eugenia. "Do you care to purchase it?"

The back door opened. Mrs. Watson came into the kitchen, followed by

Mr. Watson and the pig. "We heard the music and thought maybe you were having a party."

"We are not having a party," said Eugenia.

"Welcome, welcome," said Gaston. He smiled with his too many teeth. Mr. Watson and Mrs. Watson smiled back. They started clapping along with Frank and Baby.

The pig sat down in the middle of the kitchen floor. It grunted.

Eugenia felt dizzy with frustration. She reached out and grabbed hold of the kitchen counter to steady herself. She waited. Surely, there would be an end to the song. It could not go on forever. Could it?

When at last Gaston stopped playing, Eugenia spoke into the silence. She said, "I will ask you again. Do you wish to purchase this accordion?"

"No, no," said Gaston. "I am here only for your lessons, so you may learn to play the sweet songs and the sad songs and all the little songs in between."

"I refuse," said Eugenia.

"You refuse to learn to play the music that is waiting inside of your heart?"

"There is no music waiting inside of my heart."

"Everyone's heart has music," said Gaston. He came toward her grinning his many-toothed grin. He took the accordion from around his neck and slipped the strap over Eugenia's head.

Suddenly, she was wearing an accordion.

"Oh, Sister," said Baby. "You look marvelous."

"Inspiring!" said Mr. Watson.

"How darling!" said Mrs. Watson.

The accordion was heavy. Also, Eugenia had no interest in looking marvelous, inspiring, or darling. Everything was wrong.

Eugenia felt her face getting red.

"Miss Lincoln?" said Frank.

"I will show you," said Gaston. "You will squeeze and depress the key."

"I will not squeeze or depress the key," said Eugenia.

"Ho, ho, ho," laughed Gaston. "You will press the key and learn to play the music of your heart. That is all. That is everything." He bent toward her. He put his hands over her hands.

The man smelled like lilacs and musty curtains and butter.

Eugenia felt another wave of dizziness roll over her.

Gaston's fingers pushed her fingers down upon the keys. A small, heartbroken sound came out of the accordion. Eugenia could feel it reverberating somewhere deep inside of her.

Her heart quivered.

"You see?" said Gaston.

The kitchen became darker. Had a light gone out?

Eugenia was trembling. "I do not see," she said to Gaston.

There was a rumble of thunder from somewhere far away.

"I think it might storm," said Mr. Watson.

The kitchen became darker still.

"Let us try again," said Gaston. He wrapped his arms around Eugenia and pushed down on her fingers gently, and the song exited the accordion and entered the room.

Eugenia felt as if someone had poked her with something hot and sharp, right in the heart.

“This,” she said, “is nonsense.” She was alarmed to find that her voice was quavering. “I will not participate. I refuse to participate.”

There was a crack of thunder, a flash of lightning. The kitchen lights flickered. Eugenia took the accordion from around her neck. She handed it to Gaston. She said, “I am going to my room now.”

And that is where Eugenia Lincoln went.

She closed the door very, very firmly.

Chapter Six

Eugenia got into bed and pulled the covers over her head. But even from underneath the covers, she could hear that the accordion music and the clapping had begun again.

General Washington crept out from beneath the bed and got under the covers with Eugenia.

"Moooowwwwwwwlllllll," he said.

Eugenia could still feel Gaston's fingers on top of her fingers. She could still feel the note from the accordion reverberating in her body. It was a strange feeling.

But was it necessarily a bad feeling?

"Nonsense," said Eugenia out loud into the darkness.

And then Eugenia remembered what Frank had said: "Don't you want to know who sent you the accordion? It's very mysterious, isn't it?"

Eugenia hated to admit it, but it *was* mysterious.

It was unsettling.

Who, indeed?

The world was confusing, unpredictable, chaotic. Eugenia disapproved of confusion and unpredictability and chaos. But despite her disapproval, there still existed mysterious accordions and pigs that sat on couches and little men who wore green velvet suits.

Eugenia pulled the covers up even higher. The storm outside continued.

She could hear the rain beating down. The raindrops were so loud, so ferocious, that they almost drowned out the sound of the accordion music.

Almost, but not quite.

Underneath the covers, Eugenia put her hand on her heart.

Was there truly music in it?

"Ridiculous," said Eugenia out loud. "Geegaws, whoop-de-whoops. Frivolity."

From the kitchen, there came the sound of laughter.

Eugenia Lincoln's heart hurt just the tiniest bit.

She wasn't sure why.

In the morning, Eugenia rose from her bed and went out to the kitchen and found that it was in severe disarray: chairs were overturned, crumbs were on the counter, unwashed plates were piled in the sink. There was an entire fruitcake in the center of the kitchen table. A fly was hovering over it, buzzing happily.

"Baby!" shouted Eugenia. "I demand an explanation!"

The only answer was the buzzing of the fly.

Business cards littered the floor. The cards were covered in strange and alarming words: *taxidermy, joyous, predictions, palpitations, truffles, fleas.*

"This is unacceptable," said Eugenia.

She walked into the living room and encountered Gaston LaTreaux asleep on the couch, still wearing his velvet suit. His velvet hat was on his head. His hands were folded on his chest. There was a smile on his lips.

The accordion, that instrument of torture and chaos, was on the chair beside the couch.

"Tell me I am dreaming," said Eugenia. "Surely this is a nightmare."

Gaston's eyes fluttered. His smile deepened. He said, "Madam, I can show you. The music is within you."

Eugenia put her hand on Gaston's shoulder and shook him as violently as she dared.

His eyes remained closed. He smacked his lips and said, "Yes, the truffle, of course. The pig will be very useful in this regard."

"Wake up!" shouted Eugenia.

Gaston snuggled more deeply into the couch.

Eugenia turned her attention away from the little man.

She looked at the accordion.

Actually, she glared at it.

And horror of horrors, she felt it glaring at her in return. "You are losing your mind, Eugenia Lincoln," she said out loud. "It's time to put an end to this nonsense."

All of it—the frivolity, the chaos, the whoop-de-whoops, the little men in green suits, the music in her heart, the talking aloud to herself—all of it had to stop.

Eugenia picked up the accordion. It was very heavy, extremely heavy, entirely too heavy.

Gaston made a snuffling noise. He smacked his lips.

Eugenia looked over at him. She looked down at the accordion in her arms.

And then she tiptoed across the living room and out the front door.

General Washington followed her.

Chapter Seven

Eugenia walked east, in the direction of the rising sun, the accordion in her arms and her cat at her heels.

The light of the world was gray. A low mist clung to the ground. Eugenia had no plan.

She only knew that the accordion must be disposed of somehow.

She could put it in the trash. She could throw it in the river. She could bury it.

It would have been helpful to sit down and make a list of all the options, but there was really no time for lists, was there? She had to keep moving. Soon, Gaston would wake up. And then the chaos and the clapping and the talk of hearts (and what they held) would begin all over again.

The accordion was awkward to carry. Also, it felt like it was getting heavier. Eugenia stopped. General Washington stopped, too.

"Mooowwwwwllllll?" said the cat.

"Everything will be fine," said Eugenia. "Order will soon be restored." She put the accordion strap over her neck and the accordion immediately felt lighter, more manageable.

Eugenia walked on. General Washington stayed at her heels. The sun came up slowly, burning away the mist. And then it appeared in its entirety—whole and shining and glorious.

"Bah," said Eugenia to the sun. She continued marching east. She shaded her eyes with her hand. The question remained: What should she do with the accordion?

"Shall I burn it? Bury it? Throw it out to sea?" said Eugenia.

"Mooowwwwwlll," said General Washington in an approving kind of way.

Eugenia, too, liked the way the words sounded. She said them louder. "Shall I burn it? Bury it? Throw it out to sea?"

Truffles and butterflies and taxidermy and fleas, indeed.

She would set the world to rights.

"Burn it! Bury it! Throw it out to sea!" Eugenia shouted.

"Where are you going, Eugenia Lincoln?" someone said.

Eugenia stopped. She turned. She looked around her. The accordion let out a wheeze of surprise.

Eugenia saw no one. Was she having auditory hallucinations now? Had it come to that?

"Up here," said the voice.

Eugenia turned. The accordion squeaked.

"I'm up in the tree," said the voice.

Eugenia looked up and saw Stella, Frank's little sister, sitting in the branches of an elm tree.

"Stella Endicott," said Eugenia. "What are you doing up in that tree?"

"Thinking," said Stella. "Trees help me think. Do trees ever help you think? What are you going to do with that squeeze-box?"

"It's an accordion," said Eugenia.

"What are you going to do with that squeeze-box?" said Stella. "Are you going to burn it, bury it, throw it out to sea?"

Eugenia felt her face getting warm. "You shouldn't eavesdrop on people," she said.

"What does *eavesdrop* mean?"

"It means to listen in on other people's conversations," said Eugenia. "It's impolite. You shouldn't do it."

"You were shouting," said Stella. "I couldn't *not* hear you."

"Nonetheless," said Eugenia. "It's rude."

Stella climbed down from the tree. She said, "Can I try the squeeze-box before you burn it, bury it, throw it out to sea?"

"It's an accordion," said Eugenia.

"Can I try it?"

"I'm in a hurry," said Eugenia.

"I know," said Stella. "You're always in a hurry, Eugenia Lincoln. Can I play it?"

"Oh, for heaven's sake," said Eugenia.

"Please?" said Stella. She stood on one leg. Eugenia noticed that the child was barefoot.

"Where are your shoes?" said Eugenia.

"I'm not sure," said Stella. She looked around in a vague manner. "I think I left them somewhere. But it's fine. You don't need shoes for climbing trees, or for thinking, or for playing a squeeze-box."

"It's an accordion, and you shouldn't be running around in your bare feet," said Eugenia.

"Why not?"

"You'll catch a disease."

"You sound like Frank," said Stella. "He worries all the time, too."

"Sometimes, siblings know best," said Eugenia.

"I don't know what a sibling is," said Stella. "Can I play the squeeze-box?"

"Oh, for heaven's sake," said Eugenia. "Fine. But only for a minute."

"Goody, goody, goody," said Stella. She hopped up and down and held out her arms.

Eugenia moved to lift the accordion from around her neck, and in doing so, brushed her fingers against the keys.

A sound came forth. A sweet sound. An unexpected sound.

Eugenia froze.

"Pretty," said Stella. "Play more."

And Eugenia did.

Eugenia Lincoln closed her eyes. She squeezed the box and pushed the keys down and felt a song coming out of her. A song! How did her arms, her hands, her fingers, know what to do?

Somehow they did.

Eugenia played and Stella clapped and Eugenia's heart lifted up inside of her.

It was the most marvelous, unexpected thing that had ever happened to her. It was mysterious. It was joyous.

The sun shone down. The sky was a bright and brilliant blue.

Eugenia Lincoln played the accordion.

And when she stopped, Stella said, "You can't burn it, or bury it, or throw it out to sea, Eugenia Lincoln. You have to play and play it." She hopped from one foot to the other. "But can I try it now? Can I? Huh, huh? Can I?"

Chapter Eight

Eugenia and Stella walked back to the Lincoln Sisters' house. General Washington followed. Eugenia Lincoln was stunned, amazed. She had never been so surprised in her life.

She was a born accordion player.

Who could have known? Who could have imagined?

Baby Lincoln was in the kitchen. She was frying an egg for Gaston LaTreaux, who was sitting at the table, reading the newspaper and laughing, "Ho, ho, ho."

Coffee was percolating. The fruitcake was gone from the table. The cards had been picked up from the floor. The dishes were clean and the kitchen was filled with light.

"Sister!" said Baby. "You have returned! And good morning to you, Stella."

"Good morning, Baby Lincoln," said Stella.

"I have discovered something," said Eugenia.

"Discoveries are excellent things," said Gaston. He put down the paper. "I always celebrate discoveries. I have with me a card about the making of discoveries. One moment, please, and I will give it to you."

"I do not need a card," said Eugenia. "I have an announcement to make."

"I want a card," said Stella.

"Of course, of course, a card for you," said Gaston. "Only a moment, please." He stood and reached into his pocket and shuffled through his cards and handed one to Stella.

Tiny Miracles!

Gaston will assist you in constructing a flea circus of your very own.

Stella looked at the card. "It says that you can make a circus out of fleas. Is that true?"

"Yes," said Gaston. "It's true."

"I've never seen a circus made out of fleas."

"Gaston LaTreaux, proprietor of many tiny circuses, at your service," said Gaston. He lifted his mushroom hat from his head. He bowed to Stella.

"I said I have an announcement to make," said Eugenia. "Can no one hear me?"

"I can hear you," said Gaston.

"I can hear you, Sister," said Baby.

"Say it, say it," said Stella.

Eugenia cleared her throat. "I have discovered—" she said.

But just at that moment, Frank came in the back door and Stella said, "Guess what, Frank? Eugenia Lincoln can play a song on the squeeze-box."

"Really?" said Frank.

"Oh, Sister," said Baby. She put her hand over her heart.

Gaston said, "But of course. We knew it all along. It was written in the stars. She was born to play the accordion."

Eugenia felt annoyed. Nothing was written in the stars. Nothing was known all along.

"I will teach you what I know," said Gaston. "I will teach you all the songs. And you will practice. And you will become great—a great and happy accordion player."

The back door opened again and Mrs. Watson entered, followed by the pig. "Good morning, good morning to all," trilled Mrs. Watson.

The pig oinked.

Didn't people knock anymore? Everyone just waltzed right in the door and made themselves at home. Eugenia's happiness was evaporating. The world had not changed. Of course it had not changed. It was still the same chaotic, unpredictable, unorganized place.

"We will do great things together," said Gaston. "We will work together. But first, the pig and I must go to the woods in search of truffles."

"Truffles?" said Eugenia.

"Truffles!" said Gaston. He put his fingers to his lips and kissed them. "The mushroom of our dreams. Mercy will find them. We will go together in pursuit of the truffles, and when we return

the accordion lessons will commence."

"I am not pursuing truffles," said Eugenia.

"I want to go!" said Stella.

"So do I!" said Frank.

Soon, everyone was gone. And it was just Eugenia and General Washington and the accordion.

Eugenia stood in a patch of sun. She put her face up to the light.

What if it had been a mistake? A random occurrence? What if she *couldn't* play the accordion?

She squeezed the box. She depressed the keys, and she felt the song, again, lifting her up. It was still there!

Eugenia Lincoln stood in the kitchen and played music. Dust motes danced in the air.

She was happy.

It was the most astonishing thing.

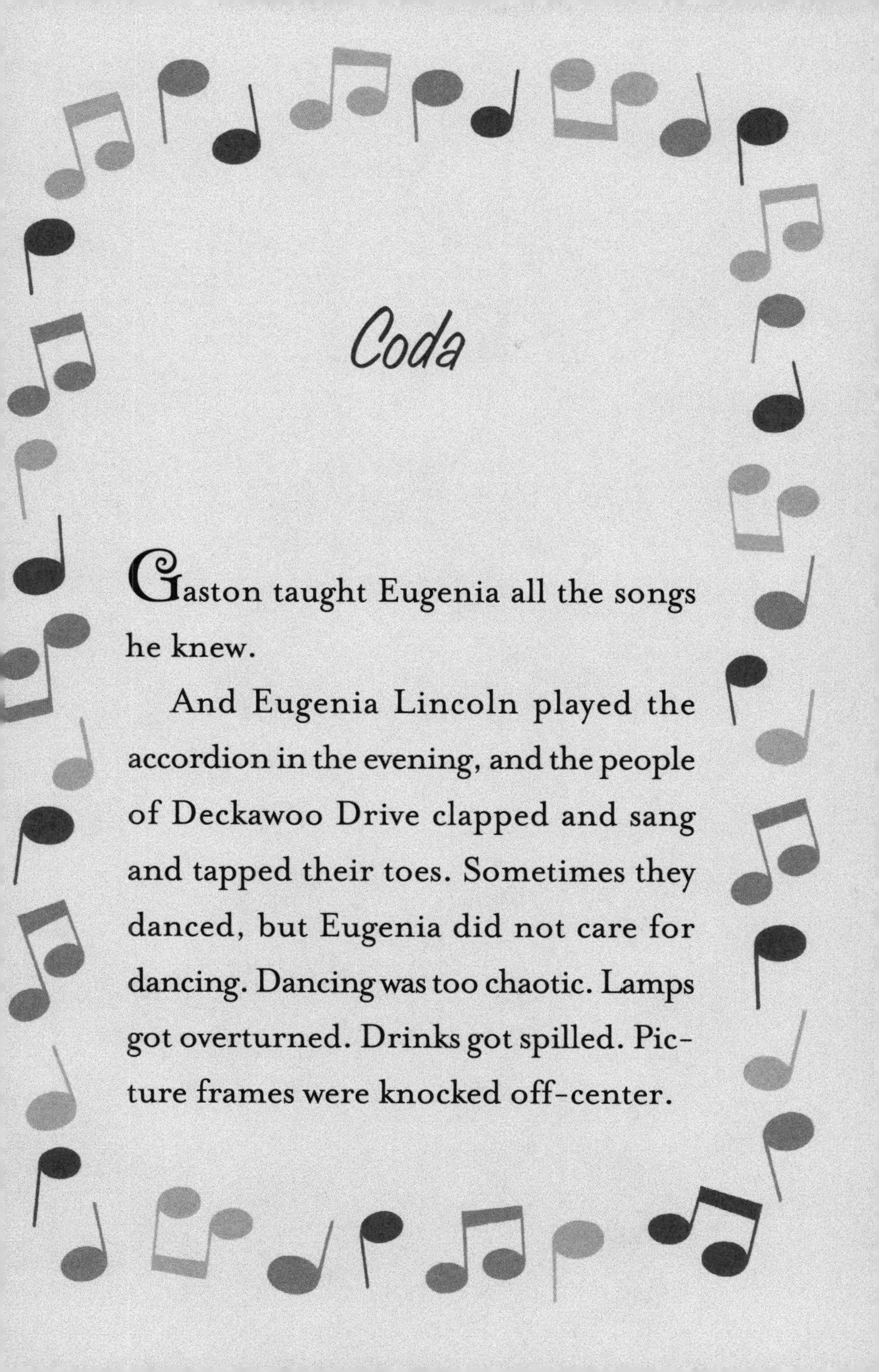

Coda

Gaston taught Eugenia all the songs he knew.

And Eugenia Lincoln played the accordion in the evening, and the people of Deckawoo Drive clapped and sang and tapped their toes. Sometimes they danced, but Eugenia did not care for dancing. Dancing was too chaotic. Lamps got overturned. Drinks got spilled. Picture frames were knocked off-center.

"Please contain yourselves," she shouted over the music.

Sometimes, they contained themselves.

And sometimes, they didn't.

One winter morning, months and months after the arrival of the unexpected package, Frank was sitting on the Lincoln Sisters' couch perusing the encyclopedia. He turned the page, and encountered the letter *J*. He turned the page again, and a piece of paper fluttered out of the encyclopedia and fell to the ground.

He bent to pick it up.

It was an ad from the Blizzintrap Schmocker Company. It said, *Great joy can be found in the accordion.*

Someone had underlined the word *joy*. And then in a shaky, hopeful hand, that someone had written: ***Perhaps for Sister?***

"Oh," said Frank.

From the kitchen came the sound of accordion music: a low, sweet tune.

"Miss Lincoln!" said Frank. "I've solved the mystery."

The accordion music stopped. Eugenia came into the living room. "Did you say something?" she said.

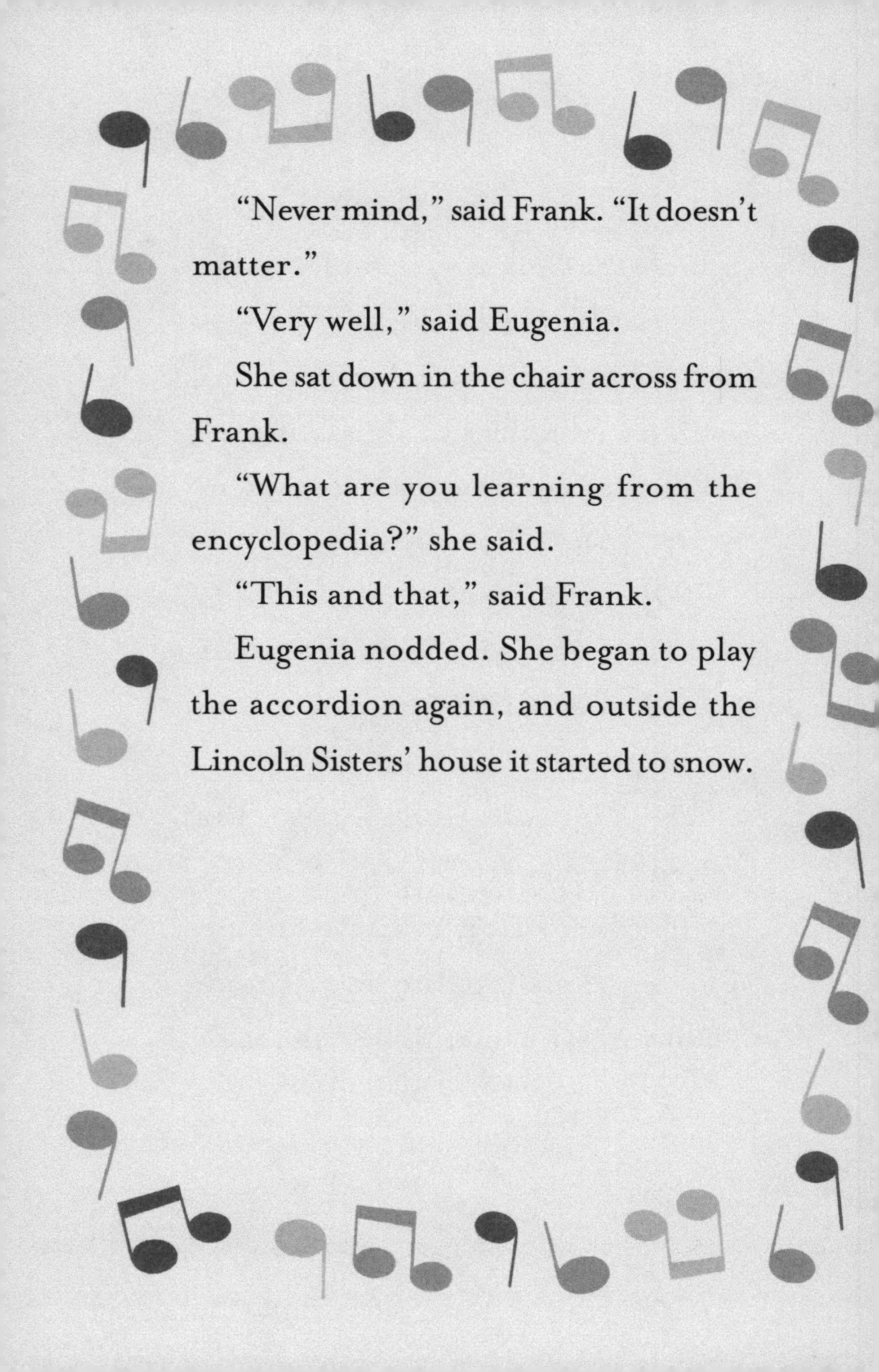

"Never mind," said Frank. "It doesn't matter."

"Very well," said Eugenia.

She sat down in the chair across from Frank.

"What are you learning from the encyclopedia?" she said.

"This and that," said Frank.

Eugenia nodded. She began to play the accordion again, and outside the Lincoln Sisters' house it started to snow.

H-J

Kate DiCamillo is the beloved author of many books for young readers, including the Mercy Watson and Tales from Deckawoo Drive series. Her books *Flora & Ulysses* and *The Tale of Despereaux* both received Newbery Medals. About *Eugenia Lincoln and the Unexpected Package,* she says, "I, like Baby, believed that there was something wondrous hiding inside Eugenia Lincoln. It was a delight to witness Eugenia's (partial) transformation." A former National Ambassador for Young People's Literature, Kate DiCamillo lives in Minneapolis.

Chris Van Dusen is the author-illustrator of *The Circus Ship, King Hugo's Huge Ego, Randy Riley's Really Big Hit,* and *Hattie & Hudson,* and is the illustrator of the Mercy Watson and Tales from Deckawoo Drive series as well as Mac Barnett's *President Taft Is Stuck in the Bath.* About *Eugenia Lincoln and the Unexpected Package,* he says, "If I were to send Eugenia Lincoln something to cheer her up, it probably wouldn't be an accordion, mainly because accordions are hard to draw (I simplified!). But it must have worked, because in this book Eugenia is actually smiling in three different illustrations. I think in the original six Mercy Watson books I only painted her smiling twice!" Chris Van Dusen lives in Maine.

Navigate a neighborhood full of mishaps, mayhem, and a lot of hot buttered toast.

www.candlewick.com